Lars the Monkey Flies a WACO Airplane

WRITTEN BY:
MEAGHAN FISHER

ILLUSTRATED BY:
MARLA FAIR

GYPSY PUBLICATIONS

Published in 2010 by Gypsy Publications
325 Green Oak Drive, Troy, OH 45373, U.S.A.

Text Copyright © Meaghan Fisher, 2010
Illustrations Copyright © Marla Fair, 2010

Lars the Monkey Flies a WACO Airplane
by Meaghan Fisher; illustrated by Marla Fair.

Summary: Lars the monkey learns to fly a WACO airplane.
ISBN 978-0-9842375-1-7 (paperback)

Book edited by Linda Gallagher
Book designed by Timothy Rowe

Manufactured in the United States of America

www.gypsypublications.com

The WACO Historical Society is located in Troy, OH.
For more information about them please visit:
www.wacoairmuseum.org

To my dear friend and editor, Linda Gallagher and a special thanks to the WACO Historical Society.

Lars was a little monkey who lived in Troy, Ohio. He was learning to fly an airplane and wanted to fly up, down, and around in loops.

Lars loved flying airplanes and today he was training with his instructor, Vince, in a WACO airplane at Troy, Ohio's Historic WACO Field. Lars wanted to learn how to give WACO airplane rides to passengers, especially children, because when he was little he loved airplane rides.

"Lars!" Vince shouted as Lars wrapped the airplane in a small loop.

"Yes, Vince!" replied Lars.

"We need to land now," Vince told Lars. "Start bringing the nose down slowly."

"Okay, I will!" shouted Lars to his instructor.

Lars landed the airplane and they both jumped out onto the grassy field.

"How was I today?" asked Lars.

"I think you were great!" replied Vince. "You will be able to fly on your own soon!"

"I will?" cried Lars happily. "That's great! I loved flying in a WACO plane when I was younger and I can't wait to show little kids how much fun it is!"

The next day was Saturday, when the Historical WACO Field airplanes performed air rides for passengers.

Lars was ready to go up for a ride when he realized he couldn't find the pilot.

Suddenly, an announcement rang through the air field: "Ladies and Gentlemen," spoke the announcer. "I am sorry to announce that Max, the WACO pilot, has fallen and hurt his wrist. Unless there is another pilot who can fly a WACO airplane, there will be no airplane rides today!"

"Oh, no!" the passengers groaned at the announcement.

"No airplane rides!" cried the children. "What will we do?"

"I can fly the plane!" Lars shouted. "I can fly it! I can conduct the airplane rides!"

"You," said the announcer, "you can fly it?" he asked Lars as he pointed at him through the crowd.

"Yes, I can do it!"

"Okay, get ready to go up," replied the announcer. "Ladies and Gentlemen, we have found a pilot!"

"Yea!" shouted the crowd of passengers with glee as Lars and his first young passenger jumped into the WACO plane.

Lars turned the airplane on and took off down the grassy runway and up into the air.

"Whee!" shouted the excited passenger as Lars flew the plane up, down, then around in small loops.

After a long ride with his passenger, Lars took the plane high into the sky and spelled out his name, "Lars," with the plane's smoke.

"Yea! We love Lars!" the crowd cheered from below as Lars landed the WACO airplane softly on the grassy runway.

After the plane stopped, Lars jumped out and helped his small passenger out of the plane.

"Thanks, Lars!" said the child as Lars helped him out of the plane and to the ground.

"It was my pleasure," said Lars to the child. "I hope you had fun!"

"I sure did!" said the child as he ran to tell his family about his WACO ride.

"Next!" Lars shouted at the line of WACO passengers in the grassy air field.

"That's me!" a small child cried out excitedly.

Lars began to help the small passenger into the plane. Then he jumped in the pilot's seat and turned on the airplane. A few minutes later, Lars and his passenger whisked down the grassy runway and flew high up into the sky.

CPSIA information can be obtained
at www.ICGtesting.com
Printed in the USA
LVIW02n1019251113
362348LV00002B/5